Down with the Dirty Danes!

Gillian Cross

Down with the Dirty Danes!

Illustrated by Tim Stevens

An imprint of HarperCollins*Publishers*

First published in Great Britain in 2000
Collins is an imprint of HarperCollins*Publishers* Ltd
77-85 Fulham Palace Road, Hammersmith, London W6 8JB

The HarperCollins website address is www.**fire**and**water**.com

1 3 5 7 9 8 6 4 2

Text copyright © Gillian Cross 2000
Illustrations by Tim Stevens 2000

ISBN 000 675534 8

The author and illustrator assert the moral right to be
identified as the author and illustrator of the work.

Printed and bound in Great Britain by
Omnia Books Limited, Glasgow

THE FIRST LETTER

From Berwin sun of Egfrith to Wulfric
sun of Elred

Dear cosen,

Yes – a letter from me! Surprise!

You dident think Id ever learn to rite did you? Nor did Mum. She thinks riteing is only for monks.

'No monking for you, Berry,' she says.

'Pleese, pleeeeeese,' I said. 'Let me be a monk and learn redeing and riteing.'

But no luck. I had to do dull stuff like fiting and digging all the time. And when there was no fiting, it was

WORSE!!

Yes, you got it. Minding the baby and looking after the gote and the geese.

NO FUN!!!

So how cum Berry is riteing a letter, I heer
you say?

Its a long story but Ill tell you.

Larst month everything was V.V. BAD heer.
Lots of misty mist and nasty news. Espeshally
– King Alfrid was being smashed to smithers by
the lowsy old Danes. The English were doing
really badly in all the fiting.

ENGLISH 0   DANES 2000

Becoz King A was losing, everywun was running out on him. Rotten swines! Whats the point of having a king if you dont stick by him?

Thats what Mum said. 'Rotten swines they are, Egfrith,' she said to my dad. 'Sumwuns got to stand by King Alfrid. Youll have to go and be in his army.'

'Me?!' said my dad. He dosent like fiting any more than me. Hees a bit of a ~~passi passyfist pasi~~ he dosent like being hit.

'Dont be a wimp, Eggy!' my mum said. 'If you dont go I will.'

That did it, of corse. Everywun nose women cant fite for toffee. Theyd trip over there skirts if they tride.

'No fiting by women!' says Dad. 'Get out my axe and stuff and Ill go and find King Alfrid. But make shore you feed the pig and the geese. And dont forget to

MILK THE GOTE.'

'Corse I wont forget,' Mum says. 'Silly old fuel!'

'You better not,' Dad says. 'And dont blame me if the Dirty Danes cum to eat the baby up while Im out helping King Alfrid.'

Ho ho ho. Everywun says the Danes eat babys, but what I say is – no such luck. If people had to cleen up babys, they wouldnt say that. Whod eat a BABY?!

Yuck, yuck, yuck!!!

So my dad took his hat and his boots and his cleen socks, and off he went, trying to look feerce and bad to scare any Dirty Danes that were abowt.

Only what did Mum find the next day? Stuck in the basket of logs by the side of the fire?

You got it!

DADS AXE!

'Oh no!' Mum says. 'When the Dirty Danes chop off his hed, he wont be able to chop them back! What can I do?'

So – what did she do?

Well, Im not telling in this letter, so HARD LUCK. My hand is **v.V.<u>V</u>.** tired and I cant rite any more. Riteing is really tuff. Im going to do sum finger X-ercises to bild up my mussels and then Ill rite anuther letter and tell you what Mum did abowt the axe.

From your cosen,
Berry

THE NEXT LETTER

Dear Wulfric,

What do you mean why was the axe in the log basket? It was for chopping logs of corse. But Dad needed it for chopping Danes. Mum went mad when she fownd it.

'Silly old fuel!' she says. 'Hows he going to kill Dirty Danes without this?'

'He could use his socks,' I say.

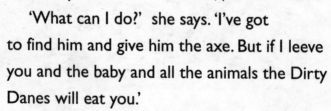

But Mums not larfing becoz shees WORRID abowt my dad.

'What can I do?' she says. 'I've got to find him and give him the axe. But if I leeve you and the baby and all the animals the Dirty Danes will eat you.'

'Weel be all rite Mum,' I say. (Going shiver shiver shiver becoz of the dirty Ds.) 'If they cum, Ill practise my fiting on them.'

'Dont be a fuel,' Mum says. 'You cant fite them on yore own. And anyway, youd let them eat the baby.' She went on cooking the dinner. Moning and groning all the time. 'What shall I do? (Boohoo boohoo.) Poor Eggy's going to get chopped to smithers by the DDs. He wont stand a chance!'

Shed just made the barley cakes and put them on the bakestone when –

NOCK! NOCK!! NOCK!!!

We look at each other and think Help Help the DDs are HEER!!

NOCK! NOCK!! NOCK!!! it goes agen.

'Who – whos there?' goes Mum.

'Pleese let me in,' says a mans voice.

Mum grabs the baby. 'Its them! Theyve cum

to eat us!!'

'Dont be stupid,' I say. 'Annywun nose Dirty Danes cant speak English.'

I open the dore. 'Hallo,' I say. 'English or Danish?' (Just checking.)

'English for ever!' he says, so I let him in.

Hees English all rite (everywun nose Danes have tails and green hair and stuff) but hees not exactly tuff. He stands in the middle of the hut going drip drip drip. (You no it always rains heer. Thats why most places are marshy and go SKWELCH. This drippy English person looks like he walked through a marsh or two. Or ten.)

'Pleese can I stay heer for the night (drip drip drip)?' he goes. 'Its wet out there.'

I thort Mum wood say 'Not on yore life. Yore a stranger.' But shees still thinking abowt Dad and the axe.

She looks at the stranger. 'What do you think of babys?'

He trys to look polite. 'There OK,' he says. 'But dogs are better.'

'You woodent eat wun?' Mum says.

The man looks at her as if shees mad.

'Good!' says Mum. 'You can stay then. But youll have to cook the dinner yoreself. And theres Berry and the baby and all the animals.'

She grabs Dads axe and opens the dore.

'Hey, hang on!' says the stranger. 'I can do dinner, but I cant do babys and gotes and geese and stuff.'

'Its OK,' says Mum. 'You look after the barley cakes. Berry can do the baby and the gote, cant you, Berry?'

I go 'Suppose so.'

'You better,' says mum. 'And dont forget to MILK THE GOTE!'

'Corse I wont!' (Dose she think Im stupid?)

'You better not,' says Mum. She puts the axe over her showlder and goes off down the path.

When shees gon I sit the baby on the flore. The man turns the barley cakes and hangs his cloke up to dry. Then he sits down by the fire. When hees stopped dripping and started steeming he takes out

A BOOK!

and he starts

REDEING!!

GASP I go. 'Yore a monk!'

'No Im not,' the man says.

'But you can do redeing!'

'So?' says the man. 'I can do riteing too.'

He bends down and dose letters in the ashes

with his finger.

BERRY

'Thats yore
name,' he says.

I copy it
underneeth his.
B E R R Y.
Its not VERY
wobbly.

'Thats rite,' the man says. 'Yore a good learner Berry.'

'My mum says only monks do redeing and riteing.'

'Yore mums a good woman,' the man says, 'but she dosent no abowt things. Everywuns got to rite. Heers some more.' He rites in the ashes agen.

DOWN WITH THE DIRTY DANES

I get exited then. I say, 'Tell me tell me pleeeeeese! Tell me all the letters.'

So he gets a bit of burnt wood out of the fire and rites the letters all over the harth in the ash.

'There you are,' he says.

I rite them myself and he makes me do them over and over agen until Ive got them all. Im getting really good when suddenly—

SSSS! SSSS!! SSSS!!!

Its the geese outside, making a fuss abowt sumthing. The man looks round.

'Wheres that baby?' he says.

I look round too.

EEEK!

The babys ~~crorled~~ ~~cralled~~ gon rite out of the dore and its out with the geese. Oh help! Mums going to kill me if they eat the baby!

So then—

I cant rite it now. My pens nerely worn out. Yorll have to wait till the next letter to see what I did abowt the baby. Riteing with worn out pens is too messy. Im going to catch a goose and make anuther wun.

From your much—cleverer—than—you— think—cosen (with BIG mussels)

Berry

LETTER NUMBER 3

Dear Wulfie,

What do you mean was the baby ~~frytenned fritent~~ scared when it was out with the geese? Of corse it was. Peck! Peck! Peck!

Geese are almost as bad as Dirty Danes for getting babys. The geese were all round the baby and it was screeming and screeming, WAAH! WAAH! WAAH!

'Oh you silly fuel!' I showt.

I run and the man runs and we go BOO and SHOO to the geese to get them away from the baby. We run them rite across the yard and shut them in the barn.

'Few!' I say. 'That was a nasty wun. Weel have to—'

But I dont get the words out becoz the man grabs my arm. 'Look there!' he says.

OH NO!!!

The babys let the pigs out and there running off into the marsh!

You no what our hut is like Wulfie – an iland with marsh all round.

Skwelch, skwelch go the pigs into the mudd and theres a huge grate SPLASH! It gets the baby smack in the face. So the babys yelling and the pigs are splashing and Im showting.

And what dose the man do? Yes, youve got
it! He goes rite into the marsh after the pigs.
Yuck, yuck, YUCK! Pigs are bad enuff
without mudd. He goes rite in up to his chest.
But he gets them out and shuts them up agen.

'Weel have to cleen the baby,' he goes. 'Babys are worse than Dirty Danes for corsing trouble.'

I pick up the baby. But then I remember what Mum said before she went.

MILK THE GOTE!!!

The gotes rememberd too, becoz it starts moning.

MAAA! MAAA!! MAAA!!!

'Weve got to do the gote,' I say. 'Itll go madd if not.'

The man goes ULP! He looks at the baby. Then he looks at the gote. Hees trying to disside which is worse. 'Ill do the gote,' he says.

So he gets the bucket and starts to milk. But hees not very good.

The gotes eating his ear, but I cant help becoz
the babys screeming and screeming. Its riggling
too, and its all slippery becoz of the mudd.

I drop it in the water troff to wosh off the mudd, but it screems worse, becoz its cold, so I leeve it dirty and get the mans cloke to rap it up.

HURRAH! SILENCE.

'Few!' says the man. He picks up the bucket. 'Ive done the gote. Now all weeve got to do is – OH!'

Its a shock. He drops the bucket and the milk goes everywhere.

'Whats up?' I say.

'Look behind you!' he wispers.

So I turn round and I see—

I SEE—

You want to no what, I bet. Well think of the most scary thing you no and MAKE IT A HUNDRED TIMES WORSE. I can't rite it becoz Im SHAKING so much.

It was – no, Ill tell you next time.

From yore cosen (hiding under the bedcuvvers),

Berry

THE FORTH LETTER

Dear Wulfie,

Of corse it wasent a hundred geese! Im not scared of geese. It was – no I cant say, it was too scary.

From,

Berry

THE FIFFTH LETTER

Dear cosen,

Of corse it wasent a gost! Im not scared of gosts. Or gotes. Or geese.

It was a grate big **WOMAN** with all brown clothes and **GREEN HAIR** hanging down all over her face and **A HUGE RED NOSE**. She had **NO ARMS** but that dident stop her being scary, becoz she had a grate big AXE − in her **MOUTH**.

And she was **RUNNING RITE AT US!**

Of corse I new it was a Dirty Dane. The DDs are so thick they dont no women cant fite. So this has got to be

A DD WOMAN!!

'Help help,' I say to the man, 'weeve got to hide! Get the gote and RUN!!!'

So hees got the gotes rope and Ive got the baby and Im showting and the gotes moning and the babys screeming and we all run into the house.

SHOUT! MAAA!! WAAAH!!!

We bar the dore and the noise gets bigger becoz the DD woman runs up and starts barging agenst it. She must have spat out the axe, becoz shees yelling and the noise is dredful.

SHOUT! MAAA!! WAAAH!!! BANG!!!! THUMP!!!!! YELL!!!!!!

I cant heer what the DD woman is yelling becoz the gotes eating the babys hair and the babys screeming in my ear and Im pulling at the gotes rope and showting 'Shut up shut up shut up Baby or the DDs will get you!'

I cant heer what annywuns saying. But suddenly I SEE. Oh no!

What do I see?

THE MAN'S UNBARRING THE DORE
TO LET IN THE DD WOMAN!

HEES A TRATOR!

Hees going to give me to the DDs! And
the baby and the gote too!!

What can I doooo?

OK, what would you have done Wulfie if
yore so clever?

asks yore cosen

Berry

THE LARST LETTER
which meens
THE END OF THE STORY

[I bet you thort it was never going to end but yore rong.]

Dear Wulfie,

No I dident hide in the log basket do you think Im wimpy or sumthing?

I hid the baby in the log basket ~~akchewly,~~ ~~acksherly~~ if you want to no. Then I got the gotes rope and ran across in front of the dore.

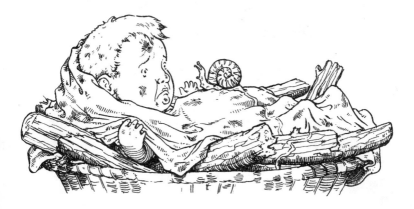

I pulled and (of corse) the gote pulled the other way. So the DD Woman ran in and went

TRIP

and then

CRASH ON THE FLORE!

She stops yelling then, becoz she looses all her breth. And the baby and the gote stop too, becoz there so surprized.

'Hurrah hurrah!' I say. 'Ive cort a Dirty Dane!'

Then I run outside and grab the axe she spat out (so she could yell). I wave the axe and showt at the man.

'Ive cort you too, you trator!' I say.
Im being reelly feerce, but Im a bit sad too becoz of the redeing and riteing).

The mans going to argew, but before he can say a word theres a grate yell from out in the garden.

'Berry! Are you there? What's going on?'

Oh hurrah hurrah hurrah! IT'S DAD!

'Dad! Dad!' I say. 'Ive cort a Dirty Dane!'

Dad runs in and gives me a big hug. 'Good thing I forgot my axe, wasent it?' he says. 'You needed it.'

His axe? Whats he on abowt? This is the DD womans axe.

But then I look agen and I see hees rite. Its got his name carved on the handel.

EGFRITH

'Oh no!' I say. 'Mum went off with this axe. If its heer – how did the DD woman get it? WHERE'S MUM?'

'Im heer, you silly fuel!'

Its the DD woman. Shees got her voice back and when she stands up I see—

OH NO!

Its Mum!

What abowt the green hair? – Marsh weed.

And the no arms? – There tide behind her bak.

And the red nose? – Its all swollen up.

Its Mum all rite, and shees **v. V. _V._** angry!

'What happened to you?' says Dad. 'You look as if you fell in a marsh.'

'I dident fall,' Mum yells. 'I was PUSHED. The Dirty Danes pushed me in the marsh!'

'WHAT?' says the man. 'Youve seen the Dirty Danes? Where were they? What were they doing?'

Hees very exited, but Mum and Dad dont even look at him becoz there too busy talking to each other.

'The Danes were PLOTTING!' Mum says. 'And I was hiding in a bush lissening. It was grate. I herd all there plans. But then a bee came and stung me on the nose. So I went OUCH!'

'You stupid fuel!' Dad said. 'Did they heer you?'

'Of corse they herd me,' Mum says. 'Danes arent def. They pulled me out of the bush and tide me up and pushed me in the marsh.'

'But you got out,' says Dad. Hees trying to carm her down but it dosent work. Mum just gets crosser.

'YES I GOT OUT!' she yells. 'ALL ON MY OWN! I EVEN GOT THE AXE FROM THE BUSH WITH MY MOUTH BECOZ I WAS TIDE UP. I STRUGGLED ALL THE WAY HOME TO GET A WOSH AND GET UNTIDE.

AND WHAT HAPPENED?'

I think I no what happened.

Oh.

'Sorry,' I say. Only in a v. small voice.

'Sorry Mum.'

Its terribul.

But its quite funny too becoz of the bogweed and her red nose and everything, so as soon as Ive said sorry I start larfing. And when I start, Dad starts. And the baby larfs too, of corse. (But not the man, becoz hees a stranger. And not the gote, becoz its a gote.)

And Mum looks as if shees going to start
larfing too, but before she can start, suddenly
theres—

SMOKE!!

And the man says, 'Oh no! Its the barley
cakes!'

Thats IT! Mum goes **ARBALLISTIC!!!**

(Arballistic is a clever word. It meens like a crossbow. Just then, Mum is like a **v.V.V.** cross bow!)

'Yore a useless stranger!' she says. 'Youve burnt the dinner!' Shees so annoyd she picks up the big pan beside the fire and hits the man round the hed with it.

'Get out get out,' she says. 'Yore worse than a Dirty Dane!'

Im shore the mans going to say it was my fault becoz of the baby and the pigs and the gote and the geese. And Mums going to go madd worse when she nose I was redeing and riteing instead of watching the baby and everything.

But the man dosent say it was my fault. He says, 'Im sorry I forgot the cakes. I was thinking.'

'THINKING!' screems Mum. 'What have you got to think abowt? Yore just a dripping man. GET OUT!'

And she hits him with the pan agen.

He cant hit her bak becoz of not fiting women so he starts making for the dore. Only he dosent get there becoz suddenly my dad looks at him and goes –

'**ITS YOU!**'

Then he grabs my mum and goes, 'You stupid fuel, its the king. Its King Alfrid and you hit him with the pan!'

'Oh no,' says Mum. 'Now heel chop off our heds!'

She falls down on her nees and starts screeming. 'Dont kill me sir. Im a mother and I have to look after all this lot becoz theyve got no sense. What will they do if you chop off my hed?'

'Dont be a fuel,' says King Alfrid. 'Im not a Dirty Dane. I dont chop off peoples heds for nothing. Annyway Ive got a much better idea.'

'You have?' says Mum. Shees even more scared now.

'Of corse I have,' says King Alfrid. 'Im the king, arent I? Having good ideas is what kings do. And Ive got a really grate idea. Its abowt yore sun Berry.'

Help! Suddenly I remember that I rapped the dirty baby in the Kings cloke. And then I put it in the log basket. And I waved Dads axe at the King.

I dont think I want to no his idea.

Mum gives a huge screem. 'Dont chop off Berrys hed! Hees a good boy even if he dosent like babys.'

'Im not going to chop off annywuns hed,' says King Alfrid. 'Why dont you—" But he dosent get to say his idea just then becoz theres anuther big noise outside. Much worse than the geese.

OINK! OINK!! OINK!!!

'Its that baby!' Mum says. 'Whats it doing to those pigs?' She pulls the dore open in a ~~fyury feeoory~~ temper.

'Mum—' I say.

Im trying to tell her it cant be the baby becoz its rapped up in the cloke in the log basket. But I cant get the words out becoz when Mum opens the dore I see sumthing terribul. Dredful.

THE WORST THING OF ALL!!!

So you can guess what that was cant you?

Yes, yore rite.

THE HOLE YARDS FULL OF DIRTY DANES!

There larfing and pulling up the cabbidges and throwing the pigs into the water troff. Which is really dirty becoz it spoils all the water.

'THATS IT!' Mum yells. 'Ive had enuff of Dirty Danes. I no women dont do fiting but sumtimes you have to do things you dont do.'

And she picks up the axe and goes charging out at the DDs.

'No! No!' showts Dad. 'Cum back you silly woman! Theyll chop you up!'

But Mums not even lissening and Dad cant go and fite too becoz he hasent got the axe. He looks round to find a weppon – and he sees the barley cakes that got burnt. There black and hard like rocks. So Dad grabs sum up and starts chucking them at the DDs, yelling 'TAKE THAT! AND THAT!'

So then I grab sum as well and so dose King Alfrid. (The baby wants wun too, but only to eat of corse.) Dad and me chuck the cakes at the DDs and we both hit wun rite on the nose.

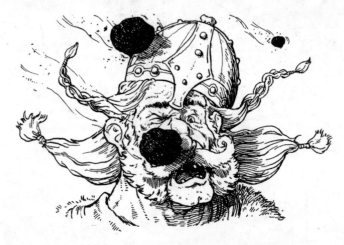

'Hurrah for Berry and Eggy!' Dad yells. 'What abowt you, Alfy?'

Then he goes wite becoz hees said Alfy to the King. But King Alfrid just larfs.

'I can do sumthing better,' he says. 'Watch this!' And he chucks a barley cake really hard.

'Missed!' Dad says. 'That was a rotten shot!'

'No it wasent,' says King Alfrid. 'Look!'

He wasent aiming at the Danes. He was
aiming at the barn – and he nocked out the peg
that holds the dore shut. So what came running
out?

You got it! GEESE!

The DDs go crazy. First they get run at by a madd woman with an axe and mudd and green hair. Then they get hit by rocks (they think). Then the geese cum out and there madder than Mum becoz they hate being shut up.

SSSSS! SSSSS!! PECK!!! PECK!!!! PECK!!!!!

King Alfrid starts yelling reelly lowd. 'Cum on men! Surround them!'

Of corse, there arnt any men, only Dad and me, but the DDs dont no that.

They think theyve run into a trap and theres a hole army waiting to tie them up and chop off there heds and thro them in the water troff. They give a grate Danish showt and start running off as hard as they can.

Im cheering and Dads cheering, but Mums really dissapointed. She tries to chase them, but of corse she cant (becoz of skirts) so she cums back in and showts at the geese instead.

'WHO LET YOU OUT?'

'It was King Alfrid with a cake!' says Dad. 'Hees really good at ~~throing throhing~~.' (He ment he could hit things with barley cakes.)

'Im better at ideas,' King Alfrid says. 'And my next idea is to get rid of all the Dirty Danes and send them home to there own country.' He grins at Mum. 'Youd better tell me what plotts you herd when you were in the bush being a spy.'

Mums really happy abowt that. She dident no she was a spy. She thort she was just a woman in a bush.

'They said there going to make a trapp for King Alfrid and his army,' she says, 'and they drew a big mapp in the mudd.'

'Did you see it?' King Alfrid says.

'Of corse I saw it,' says Mum.

King Alfrid looks really pleesed. 'Can you draw it?'

'Of corse,' says Mum.

She goes over to the harth, to draw the mapp in the ashes. But then she sees the letters I did when King Alfrid was teaching me.

'WHOSE BEEN RITEING IN MY FIRE??' she says.

Im scared shees going to be cross, but King
Alfrid says, 'Oh, that was Berry.'

'BERRYS BEEN DOING RITEING?'

'Yes,' says King A. 'Hees a good fire-riter.
Thats why I had my idea abowt him.'

Oh no! Not the idea! I thort heed forgotten
abowt that! Im really scared I can tell you. I get
the baby and pull off the cloke.

'Im sorry abowt the cloke,' I say as fast as I
can. 'Ill wash it I promise! And Im sorry abowt
waving the axe at you. Dont chop off my hed!
Pleeese!'

'Of corse Im not going to chop off yore hed,'
King Alfrid says, as if Im really stupid. 'Im going let
you cum to my skool.'

'Skool?' I say.

'Skool?' says Mum.

'Skool,' says King A. 'Im going to start wun when Ive got rid of all the Dirty Danes. Berry can cum to it and learn redeing.'

Mum gives him a look.

'Oh and riteing,' King Alfrid says.

Mum gives him a worse look but she cant do annything becoz of him being the king ha ha ha. So she says 'Yes sir!'

'Oh and Latin,' says King Alfrid. 'Then he can be a person who works for me.'

'Latin?' says Mum. Thats different becoz only important people do Latin. She starts smiling and you can tell shees really happy. Shees thinking she can tell everywun in the village that King Alfrid came to dinner and hees going to take her sun to work for him.

And thats what she did. She went on and on abowt it until everywun in the village was sick of it. Then sumwun asked her what she gave King A to eat and she shut up v. fast.

So thats it, Wulfie. Im going to the Kings skool
and Im going to do redeing and riteing and Latin.
Ive been practissing all over the village riteing

KING ALFRID IS GRATE!

and

DOWN WITH THE DIRTY DANES!!

Redeing is harder becoz I cant rede anything

heer except what I do myself. Pleese rite me a letter soon Wulfie, becoz Im tired of redeing the walls heer.

Your riteing—without—monking cosen,

Berwin sun of Egfrith

PS I no sum Latin too becoz King A told me sum.

MAGNUS EST REX ALFREDUS!
and
VAE SORDIDIS DANIS!!

PPS Whats rong with being a monk annyway?

Order Form

To order direct from the publishers, just make a list of the titles you want and fill in the form below:

Name ....

Address ....

....

....

Send to: Dept 6, HarperCollins Publishers Ltd, Westerhill Road, Bishopbriggs, Glasgow G64 2QT.

Please enclose a cheque or postal order to the value of the cover price, plus:

UK & BFPO: Add £1.00 for the first book, and 25p per copy for each additional book ordered.

Overseas and Eire: Add £2.95 service charge. Books will be sent by surface mail but quotes for airmail despatch will be given on request.

A 24-hour telephone ordering service is available to holders of Visa, MasterCard, Amex or Switch cards on 0141- 772 2281.

Collins
An *Imprint of* HarperCollins*Publishers*